AND THE AWFUL EAR WACKS ATTACKS

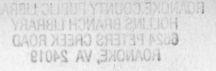

ZONDERKIDZ

Larryboy and the Awful Ear Wacks Attacks
Copyright © 2002 Big Idea, Inc. VEGGIETALES®, character names, likenesses and other indicia are trademarks of Big Idea, Inc. All rights reserved.

Requests for information should be addressed to:

Zonderkidz, *Grand Rapids, Michigan 49530*

Library of Congress Cataloging-in-Publication Data
Katula, Bob.
  Larryboy and the awful ear wacks attacks / written by Bob Katula.
     p. cm.
"Based on the hit video series: Larryboy. Created by Phil Vischer.
Series Adapted by Tom Bancroft."
"Big Idea."
Summary: Larryboy, a heroic cucumber with plunger ears, comes to the rescue when Alvin the Onion unleashes the awful ear wacks to interfere with being a good listener.
"Zonderkidz."
  ISBN 978-0-310-70468-3 (pbk.)
 [1. Heroes—Fiction. 2. Cucumbers—Fiction. 3. Vegetables—Fiction. 4. Listening—Fiction.] I. Larryboy. II. Title.
  PZ7.K15668 Lar 2002
  [Fic]—dc21

                                                                    2002012698

Written by: Bob Katula
Editor: Cindy Kenney, Gwen Ellis, and Kent Redeker
Cover and Interior Illustrations: Michael Moore
Cover Design and Art Direction: Paul Conrad, Karen Poth, and Jody Langley
Interior Design: Holli Leegwater, John Trent, and Karen Poth

Printed in the United States of America

10 11 12 13 14 15 16 /DCI/ 26 25 24 23 22 21 20 19 18 17 16 15 14 13

AND THE AWFUL EAR WACKS ATTACKS

WRITTEN BY
BOB KATULA

ILLUSTRATED BY
MICHAEL MOORE

BASED ON THE HIT VIDEO SERIES: LARRYBOY
CREATED BY PHIL VISCHER
SERIES ADAPTED BY TOM BANCROFT

TABLE OF CONTENTS

CHAPTER 1

THE GIANT SLIME MONSTER

It was an average day in Bumblyburg. The leaves were rustling on the trees, the birds were perched on the statues in the park, and Bumblyburg's own superhero, Larryboy, was on patrol.

Larryboy was slowly driving the Larry-Mobile around the city, looking for signs of crime or other superhero-needing situations. Normally, Larryboy liked going on patrol. But today, he was bored.

"I am sooo bored!" he said. "There's nothing happening today … except for the situation with the birds and the statues. But I'm not going to intervene in that! If I don't see some sorta trouble soon, I'm gonna go home and make myself a big peanut-butter sandwi…"

The Larry-Mobile screeched to a halt. Larryboy saw something coming over the hill, and he couldn't believe his eyes.

A great big slimy purple blob was creeping over the hill, wiggling menacingly as it came.

"Oh, peanut brittle!" said Larryboy. "It's a

giant purple slime monster!!"

Right then, Larryboy would have attacked the giant purple slime monster in an effort to save Bumblyburg from its vicious slimy attacks. He would have attacked, except for one thing: Larryboy was scared of giant purple slime monsters.

So instead, Larryboy parked the Larry-Mobile and jumped into the bushes to hide as the giant purple slime monster came over the hill.

"Bumblyburg is doomed!" Larryboy thought to himself. "We need a superhero or something to stop it!"

Then, with horror, Larryboy realized something. "Wait ...I...am...that...hero. Drat."

Even though he was afraid, he had to try to stop the giant purple slime monster. Bumblyburg depended on him!

So, as the giant purple slime monster passed the bushes where Larryboy was hiding, he closed his eyes, gritted his teeth, and fired one of his plunger ears.

"Hey!" said the giant purple slime monster. "I've been plungerized!"

This startled Larryboy. He didn't expect the giant purple slime mon- ster to talk. Besides, it didn't sound *anything* like a giant purple slime monster should sound.

"Help! Get this plunger off me! I can't see!" it said.

Then Larryboy realized something: The giant purple slime monster didn't sound like a giant purple slime monster. It sounded like Wally!

Larryboy looked up from behind the bushes, and this is what he saw: Herbert and Wally carrying the largest plate of grape-flavored gelatin he had ever seen.

Larryboy rushed from the bushes and released Wally from his plunger ear. Herbert and Wally explained that they had filled the city swimming pool with grape gelatin, and now they were taking the whole thing home to eat. They didn't even seem to mind that there was a pair of swim fins and a life preserver suspended in the middle of the giant gelatin mold.

"Wow," said Larryboy. "That's a lot of gelatin!"

CHAPTER 2

MUSHROOM AMUCK

This would have probably been the yummiest day of Herbert and Wally's life, except for what happened next.

As Larryboy stood admiring the huge purple blob of gelatin, young Angus Mushroom zoomed up on a scooter, going way too fast!

"Coming through!" shouted Angus.

Larryboy jumped out of the way just in time. But when he jumped aside, he bumped into Wally, causing the giant gelatin to wobble and jiggle dangerously.

"WHOOOOOOAH!" said Herbert and Wally as they tried not to drop the wiggly purple glob.

"Hold on!" said Larryboy. "If I can just activate my gelatin stabilizer device ..."

But it was too late. Herbert and Wally lost control of the gelatin and dropped it right on Larryboy. Larryboy

was a sticky, purple mess. On top of that, he was stuck in a life preserver.

"Are you okay?" asked Herbert.

"Of course I'm okay," said Larryboy. "It takes more than getting mucked up with gelatin to stop a super-hero! But Angus Mushroom might cause more accidents if I don't stop *him*!"

Larryboy got up and hopped over to the Larry-Mobile where he pulled out a rocket-powered skateboard and a helmet. "Traffic violation! This is a job for the Larry-Board!" he said.

With that, Larryboy, covered in purple gelatin and with a life preserver around his waist, hopped onto the skateboard and took off after Angus. Problem was, Larryboy wasn't so good at skateboarding.

"WHOOOOAH DOGGIE!" he said as he whooshed after Angus.

In seconds, the rocket-powered Larry-Board caught up to Angus, and Larryboy rode beside him. "Stop! Stop!" said Larryboy.

"Scott?" said Angus with a confused expression. "My name's Angus, not Scott."

"I know," said Larryboy. "But you have to..."

WHAM!

Larryboy was so busy trying to get Angus to stop that he didn't notice Pa Grape walking along the sidewalk carrying a barrel of Mexican jumping beans. Larryboy crashed into the barrel, sending jumping beans everywhere…including down his spandex superhero suit.

"Hey!" said Pa Grape. "You spilled my jumping beans!"

"Sorry," said Larryboy, "but I gotta go stop Angus before he causes more accidents."

So, Larryboy got back on his Larry-Board and zoomed off after Angus, covered in gelatin, a life preserver around his tummy, and Mexican jumping beans in his suit.

Larryboy caught up to Angus and his scooter again. "Halt!" he said.

"Malt?" said Angus. "I'd love a chocolate malt!"

"No, no," said Larryboy.

WHAM!

Again, Larryboy wasn't looking where he was going. So he didn't see the big hat display out front of the lady's clothing store. He crashed right into it, sending hats everywhere…including a big flowery one that landed on his head.

But Larryboy knew he had to stop Angus before he caused any more accidents. So he kept on going…covered in grape gelatin, a life preserver around his waist, Mexican jumping beans in his suit, and a lady's hat on his head that covered his eyes.

Then he ran smack into a wall.

"Ouch," he said.

Fortunately for Larryboy, Chief Croswell had volunteered to fill-in for the school crossing guard that day. He was just about to help Junior Asparagus cross the street when he saw Angus coming on his scooter, going way too fast. Chief Croswell held up his 'stop' sign and yelled, **"STOP!"**

Angus read the 'stop' sign and finally came to a stop.

"Why does everyone keep calling me Scott?" he asked.

Moments later, Larryboy rocked up on the Larry-Board...and ran into a mailbox.

"Ouch," he said.

By now, the jumping beans in his suit were really starting to tickle. He leapt off his Larry-Board and began jumping around as if his suit was on fire.

Chief Croswell and Junior Asparagus looked at Larryboy who was jumping around wildly, covered in purple gelatin, wearing a life preserver around his waist and a lady's hat on his head. "Are you okay, Larryboy?" Junior asked.

"Yeah," said Larryboy. "Why do you ask?"

CHAPTER 3

TAFFY, BUT NO LAFFY

As Chief Croswell tried to sort things out, a dark figure watched from a nearby alley, doing his best to cloak himself in darkness.

This dark figure was Larryboy's arch enemy, Awful Alvin the Onion, a tall, thin stalk of a villain with a bulbous head. He peered through a monocle under one of his bushy eyebrows, but noticed the light on behind him.

Awful Alvin turned to his henchman, Lampy, who was...well, a floor lamp. "Turn off your light, Lampy!" said Awful Alvin. "You'll give away our location!"

Lampy didn't respond, so Awful Alvin reached over and switched Lampy's light off himself.

"We can't let Larryboy and Chief Croswell see us now. After all, the test on Angus Mushroom worked perfectly! Soon I shall be able to unleash my *awful* plan! Then Larryboy and all of Bumblyburg will be listening to me and only me! HA HA HA HA HA HA HA!"

For some reason, Lampy didn't laugh along.

Half an hour later, Angus's mother, Gladis Mushroom, arrived to take her son home. Angus was waiting with Chief Croswell and Larryboy, who kept jumping around and bumping into walls with a lady's hat still on his head.

"Are you okay, Larryboy?" asked Gladis.

"Of course!" said Larryboy. "Why does everyone keep asking me that?"

Chief Croswell turned to Gladis. "We're glad you're here," he said. "We've been questioning Angus for half an hour, but he won't tell us why he was riding his scooter so recklessly. He just won't listen to us!"

Gladis looked at her son with a frown that let Angus know he was in big trouble. "Why do you look so mad?" asked Angus. "I was only doing what you told me to do."

"What are you talking about?" she said.

"You said, 'Take your scooter and play in traffic!'" said Angus.

"I said no such thing!" said Gladis. "I said, 'Get some sugar for making taffy.'" She turned to Chief Croswell and said, "I love to make taffy! My specialty is chicken-flavored taffy!"

Larryboy, who was still covered in purple gelatin, wearing a life preserver around his tummy and a lady's hat on his head, and still had pants full of jumping beans, tripped and fell into a puddle.

CHAPTER 4

GIVE ME A HOME
WHERE THE COCKROACHES ROAM

Before we go any further with our story, we should probably go back and talk about Awful Alvin. You need to know how truly *awful* he is.

Awful Alvin, like any other villain worth his weight in doomsday dungarees, had a secret underground lair. Awful Alvin's particular secret underground lair was a humble, starter lair on the outskirts of Bumblyburg. It was a pretty bad neighborhood, but not quite as awful as Awful Alvin would have liked. Something to work up to, he thought. The roaches and vermin made it feel like home, though, so Awful Alvin had put out his "Unwelcome" mat and settled in.

Second-hand computers and lame lab equipment surrounded him. The kind of stuff you grew tired of

when you were six. Still, by keeping the lights low and never cleaning, Awful Alvin was able to create a creepy enough setting for villainy and outdated computer games.

Lights flashed, liquids bubbled, turbines whirred, generators chugged, and an array of devices blipped and chirped a language all their own. Not to mention, something behind the refrigerator really stunk!

By Awful Alvin's side stood his faithful partner in crime, Lampy. During his years of villainy, Awful Alvin had been so awful that he had driven away all his friends. Like the time in the tropics when he replaced Apple

Strudel's sunscreen with olive oil and burned his light and flaky crust. Or the time when he scared the Pumpkin Brothers half to death by filling their beds with fake seeds and orange Silly String while they slept.

After a while, Lampy was the only one who seemed to be able to put up with him.

"Lampy!" said Awful Alvin as they returned to their lair. "The test was a success! The Ear Wacks worked perfectly!"

Awful Alvin held up a small velvet box and opened the lid. He reached in and took out a tiny blinking gadget, no larger than a ladybug. But it wasn't a ladybug. It was an

Ear Wack. Taking a ladybug out of the box at this point would make absolutely no sense whatsoever.

"Who would ever think such a small, unnoticeable thing as my Ear Wacks could interfere with something so important as listening?" Alvin pondered.

The first part of his evil plan had worked to perfection when he had slipped the first pair of experimental Ear Wacks into Angus Mushroom's bedroom the night before. He placed the box beside Angus's bed and left a note reading, "Hey, kid! Tired of always having to listen to adults telling you what do? Then try these new Ear Wacks! You'll be able to fool your parents and teachers into thinking that you're listening, when actually, you'll only hear what you *want* to hear!"

This sounded just great to Angus, and he eagerly put the Ear Wacks into his ears. Instantly, he began hearing only what he *wanted* to hear.

When his mom scolded, "Angus! You're late for breakfast," Angus heard, "Angus, you're great for being so fast!"

As he headed out the door for school, his mom called, "Honey, be sure to get some sugar for making taffy!" And, as you already know, what Angus heard was, "Honey, be sure to take your scooter and play in traffic!"

The Ear Wacks had worked perfectly! Not only had Angus heard what he wanted to hear and nothing more, but the Ear Wacks also caused him to ride his scooter recklessly, which caused Larryboy to end up with a lady's hat on his head.

Things couldn't have gone any better if Awful Alvin had planned it that way. Of course, he *had* planned it that way. So, in his final analysis, Awful Alvin had to conclude that things could not have gone any better.

But this was only the beginning. Angus was a small potato (or, more accurately, a small mushroom). Awful Alvin was after the *big* prize now. He was after Larryboy! And when he caught the superhero, Awful Alvin had something *especially* awful planned.

"Behold the Extreme Ear Wacks, Lampy!" From a very large box, Awful Alvin carefully lifted two glowing objects. The softball-sized orbs pulsed orange, like hot metal, and caused a slight tremor in the air.

"When these are placed in the super-suction ears of that purple pretender, Larryboy will have to listen to me, and only ME, for the rest of his days!" Awful Alvin put the Extreme Ear Wacks back in their box and began laughing. **"HA HA HA HA HA!** My plan is so brilliant that if I hadn't come up with it myself, I wouldn't have believed that someone could come up with a plan so brilliant! But I, Awful Alvin, am brilliant! *Awfully* brilliant! So I do believe it! I do! I do! **HA HA HA HA!"**

CHAPTER 5

COFFEE ANYONE?

Later that day, Bob the
Tomato sat at his desk, sipping coffee
from his "World's Sauciest Editor" mug,
and thinking of all the reasons that it was
really fun to be editor of the *Daily Bumble*
newspaper. "Reason number thirty-six...I can
have all the hot coffee I want! Reason number thirty-
seven...If I had feet, I could put them up on my
desk, and no one would tell me I couldn't! Reason
number thirty-eight...I can sit around thinking of use-
less lists, and it looks like I'm working..."

Just then, Junior Asparagus burst into his office.

"Editor Bob!" said Junior.

"Waaaa!" said Bob, as he awoke from his daydreaming. He was so startled by Junior that he
knocked over the cup of steaming hot coffee on his
desk. "Oh, no! Can somebody get Larry, the janitor,
in here?" he yelled. Then, he looked back at
Junior. "Junior Asparagus! Haven't I told you
never to burst into my office while I'm day-
dream...um...working!?"

"Well, yeah," said Junior. "But I've got a really great lead on a story! You see Angus Mushroom wasn't listening to his mother and…"

Bob jumped in without listening. "Wait a minute! Since when is it news when a kid doesn't listen to his mother? It happens every day. Why it happens every minute! Right now, somewhere in Bumblyburg, some kid's not listening," Bob continued without letting Junior get a word in edge-wise. "I've tried to explain this before, Junior. When a dog bites a person, that's *not* news. It happens every day. When a person bites a dog, *that's* news! It hardly ever happens. Except with my Grandpa Ed and his dog, Rusty. But that's the exception! I'm not going to cover a story about kids not listening. I can't! I hope you understand."

Junior sulked out of Bob's office. He *knew* there was more to this story. He decided that he couldn't give up! He hadn't given up when he was writing stories for the *Bumblyburg Elementary Reader*. His determination allowed him to break the big story on suspiciously shorter recesses. And he had to work hard to get some of his other stories published, such as "Turbocharge Your Gerbil Wheel," the much talked about article that explained how to popularize motor sports with domestic rodents.

Junior decided that this not-listening story had to be covered! He decided right then and there that he would go interview Angus Mushroom…right after school.

Back in his office, Bob the Tomato was getting redder by the minute. He was extremely annoyed that Larry wasn't in

his office yet. He was just about to place an ad for a new
janitor when he heard the voice of Gladis Mushroom.

"Yoo hoo!" she said.

"Mrs. Mushroom?" said Bob. "What are you doing here?"

"Well, I just made a batch of my famous chicken-flavored
taffy, and I was wondering if you wanted some."

"Well, I…" said Bob just as Larry rushed into the room.

"I got here as soon as I could, Bob!"

"Finally!" Bob groaned.

"What is it, Bob? One of the printing presses needs its
thingamabob adjusted? A massive roll of newsprint is off its
doohickey? The folding mechanism all cattywumpus?" Larry
couldn't wait to actually fix something.

"No, it's coffee," Bob said, pointing to the site of the spill.
"That mop should do the trick. Now, while you clean up, I'm
gonna go have some taffy!"

CHAPTER 6

SPEAK SOFTLY
AND CARRY A BIG MOP

Larry was cleaning up the last of the coffee spill when his mop handle began to vibrate. "I think my mop has had a little too much caffeine," he thought. Then he remembered that his trusted friend and butler, Archie, had installed a digital communications device into the mop handle so he could contact Larryboy when necessary.

"Hello, Master Larry," Archie said. "Can you hear me?"

"Yes, Archie," Larry answered, speaking into the mop handle. But he couldn't find the handy video screen. "You're coming in loud and clear! This thing is so cool. It's the best thing to hit the janitorial world since blue toilet water!"

"Hello? Master Larry, are you there?" Larry could hear Archie, but it was apparent that Archie could not hear Larry.

"Are you talking directly into the mop?" Archie said. "You need to speak directly into it."

Now Larry remembered. He was supposed to turn the mop upside down and talk directly into

it. But the bottom of his mop was in the bucket, and the bucket had coffee in it. Larry looked around Bob's office and found a "World's Sauciest Editor" mug and poured the coffee into it.

Then he flipped the bucket and mop over his head and stuck his head into it. "Archie! Can you hear me now?" Larry shouted.

Larry's voice boomed into the headphones that Archie was wearing, causing him to grit his teeth into a distorted grin. "Master Larry," Archie said with a sigh, "take the bucket off your head. It creates quite an echo."

Larry lifted the bucket off his head, which allowed the screen to come into focus. "There you are!"

"Master Larry, I just wanted to remind you about your superhero class tonight at the Bumblyburg Community College. I'll see you right after class."

"Really? Will you be in the hall when I come out of

class?" Larry asked.

"No, I'll be here, at home," Archie replied.

"So technically, you won't see me right after class," Larry said with a frown.

"Technically, no," Archie agreed.

"Because even in good traffic with the Larry-Mobile, I may not get there until..."

"I understand," Archie interrupted. "I'll see you moments after you arrive home."

"Really? Will you be waiting for me at the door?" Larry asked.

"Perhaps you should get back to your janitorial duties, Master Larry," Archie said. "Before you arouse suspicion."

"Oh, right, Archie! Toodles!" Larry said, switching off the mop before he went back to cleaning Bob's office.

CHAPTER 7

THE EAR WACKS UNRAVELS

Junior Asparagus was a determined reporter. He always got his story. But this story was really testing the limits of his patience. He had been sitting in Angus Mushroom's bedroom for half an hour, and he wasn't getting *anywhere*! Angus just plain wasn't listening to any of his questions!

Junior tried again. "What's causing your listening problem?" he asked for the tenth time.

"I told you," said Angus. "I'm not pausing to do a whistling album!"

Junior beat his head against his reporter's notebook. "No, no, no! That's not what I said at all! I've asked the same question every time! Look, I've even got it written down right here!" Junior held the notebook up to Angus and showed him the question.

This time, Angus seemed to understand. "I don't have a listening problem! But I do have something really cool. It's my new Ear Wacks!"

"EWWW! GROSS!" Junior said, scrunching up his nose. But then, Junior realized something: Angus was having trouble listening, but he could *read* just fine!

"Mom was really mad when I got home," said Angus. "She made me wash my ears out real good. I even had to take my Ear Wacks out! But I put 'em back in when I was done."

Junior winced at the thought of ear wax being yanked out of and put back into someone's ears. He wrote another question on the paper and showed it to Angus.

WHY WOULD YOU WANT TO DO THAT?

"So I can hear whatever I want to!" Angus said. "It was easy. I just reached in and pulled the Ear Wacks right out! Then I stuck them right back in again."

Junior, normally not squeamish, was getting a little greener around the stalk. But he knew a good reporter didn't let his feelings get in the way, so he wrote another question.

IT CAME OUT IN ONE BIG CHUNK?

"No, it's little," said Angus. "Want to see it?"

Junior nodded nervously, not really wanting to look. But when Angus showed him the small blinking Ear

Wacks devices, his reporter's instincts took over.

"What are *those*?"

"Ear Wacks!" Angus said again. "Like I've been telling you all along."

He showed Junior the box they came in, and Junior read

the note that came with them: "Hey, kid! Tired of always having to listen to adults tell you what do? Then try these new Ear Wacks! You'll be able to fool your parents and teachers into thinking that you're listening, when actually, you'll only hear what *you* want to hear!"

Now Junior under-stood! Those gizmos were called Ear *Wacks*. It wasn't ordinary ear wax that was causing the listening problem. It was Ear Wacks!

"Where did they come from?" Junior asked, and then listened as Angus explained that they were right on the table next to the open window when he woke up that morning. Someone had planted them there while he slept!

"So you don't hear anything with them in?"

"Only when you don't want to," Angus said, putting them back in. "You only hear what you *want* to hear!"

Junior stopped to think about what this meant. He

thought about all the times that kids didn't want to listen to something important! Directions, rules, guidance, and all sorts of information that came from teachers, parents, doctors...even God! Where would it end?

It would be very tempting to just stop listening to what you didn't want to hear. But the consequences could be disastrous! Junior knew that Ear Wacks were a serious threat to Bumblyburg, and he had to stop them from getting into anyone else's ears.

Junior turned the box over to see if there was anything else written on it. On the bottom, he noticed the initials M.M.

"M.M.!" Junior shouted.

Just then, Gladis Mushroom popped her head in the door. "Anyone want some taffy?"

"You bet!" said Angus. His ears worked just fine when it came to hearing about taffy. But Junior Asparagus knew *he* had no time for taffy.

"Thanks, Mrs. Mushroom, but I've got to get this down to the *Daily Bumble* right away so I can warn everyone about this mysterious M.M. before he plants any more Ear Wacks!"

Junior rushed out of the room leaving Mrs. Mushroom with a confused expression. "Why would anyone want to plant ear wax?"

CHAPTER 8

AN EAR-REGULAR STORY

Bob the Tomato was heading down the hall on his way back to his office at the *Daily Bumble*. As he walked along, he was daydreaming again. This time, he was thinking about how much fun it would be to play in a pool filled with grape gelatin. You could bounce all over the place, play bouncy bowling, turn somersaults, and...

"Editor Bob!" Junior yelled as he burst into the *Daily Bumble* building.

"Waaaa!" said Bob as he once again broke out of his daydreaming.

Junior rushed up to Bob, "I've got big news! Ear Wacks are what's prevented Angus Mushroom from listening!"

"Ear wax?" Bob replied. **"EEEWWW!** Isn't that a little ear-regular?" He chuckled at his own little joke. "Well, I'm glad we got to the bottom of *that* big story!"

"No, you don't understand," Junior persisted. "It *is* a big story!

We have to warn people before everyone has Ear Wacks!"

"Junior, I think most folks already have ear wax," Bob said with a grin. "I'm afraid that's not a good enough story for the *Daily Bumble*. Now if you'll excuse me, I've got some important daydrea…I mean work to do!"

Bob went back to his office and was pleased to see Larry working. The coffee spill had been cleaned up. *Wow,* he thought, *Larry even brought me a new cup of coffee!* He walked over and took a big gulp from his "World's Sauciest Editor" mug, not knowing that he was about to drink a fresh cup of squeezed mop.

"Something wrong, Bob?" asked Larry. "You're looking a little green…and that's unusual for *you.*"

Bob didn't respond. He was too busy feeling ill.

Larry shrugged and walked out into the hall, where he ran into Junior Asparagus. "What's up, Junior?" he asked.

"I've got to think of a way to convince Bob that there's a serious threat to Bumblyburg!" Junior insisted. "And I'm not talking about the return of polyester."

"Um…Bob doesn't seem to be talking to anyone just now," Larry said. "Why don't you tell me about it?"

"It's right here in this box," Junior said, taking out the small box labeled "Ear Wacks." "It's the Ear Wacks that came out of Angus Mushroom's ears."

"EEEWWW!" Larry said, wrinkling his nose.

"No, look!" Junior said, opening the box.

"EEEWWW! EAR WAX!" Larry said, wrinkling his entire face and hiding behind his mop. Then he peeked around the mop strands and saw the two blinking dots, like electronic ladybugs. "Ooooo! That's pretty cool!"

For the next five minutes, Larry listened with rapt attention as Junior told him what he had learned about the Ear Wacks and the M.M. initials. He told Larry how important it was to warn everyone before the Ear Wacks got out to the general public.

"This sounds like a job for Larryboy!" Larry said, striking a heroic pose.

"Yeah!" Junior said, smiling at the janitor's sudden goofiness. "Someone should tell him!"

"I am that *someone*!" Larry said. Now he was thinking like Larryboy! This had to be the work of one of his arch-enemies. But he couldn't think of anyone with the initials M.M., other than former NBA star, Moses Malone. Larry was pretty sure it wasn't him. He knew he had to get a pair of Ear Wacks to Archie for analysis.

"Could I have those?" Larry asked Junior, taking the Ear Wacks. "I have some equipment in my janitor's closet that could give us some answers. You'd be surprised what I can do with a good plunger and some duct tape. Don't worry, Junior. I'll take it from here."

Junior reluctantly agreed. "Okay, but if your equipment doesn't work, be sure to get it in the hands of Larryboy!"

"Will do!" Larry shouted as he disappeared around the corner.

CHAPTER 9

A CLASS ACT

After Larryboy got the Ear Wacks to Archie, he went on to his superhero class at the Bumblyburg Community College. The classroom was filled with a colorful assortment of costumes that concealed the true identities of the superheroes.

Just as Bok Choy, the teacher of the class, made his way to the front of classroom, Larryboy's belt buckle began beeping. All of the superheroes looked at their belts to see if their belt radios were beeping.

"Mine!" Larry said as he got up to step out into the hall. "Sorry, for the interruption fellas, but I'm gonna have to take this. Superhero stuff, ya know."

"Yo! Larryboy speaking."

"Master Larry, it's Archie."

"Well, of course it's you, Archie. Nobody else has this number," Larry said.

"I've determined that the Ear Wacks have a tiny microchip that somehow interferes with the user's

ability to listen," Archie said. "And according to the computer, the initials 'M.M.' seem to stand for Masked Messenger."

"Aha! Then it's *not* Moses Malone!"

"No. I'm afraid you'll have to look elsewhere for this Masked Messenger."

"He could be hard to spot. He might be wearing a *mask*," Larryboy said.

"Correct. That means he could even be in your class posing as a superhero," Archie pointed out. "Be on your toes, Master Larry!"

Larryboy looked down, a little confused about how he could do that. "Wow! A villain in superhero class! Wait until I tell the other superheroes! They'll be so excited!"

"No, Master Larry!" Archie said. "You can't let the Masked Messenger know you're on to him. Say nothing to anyone!"

There was no response. Archie waited a moment until he realized that Larryboy was taking his advice a little too literally. "I mean say nothing to anyone in *class*," Archie clarified.

"Oh," said Larryboy.

Bok Choy was already speaking as Larryboy returned to the class-room. "So if you'll turn in your *Superhero Handbook* to Section 20, Paragraph 1, Line 5, we come to today's lesson: 'Let the wise listen and add to their learning, and let the discerning get guidance.'"

Larryboy stood in the doorway and scanned the class-room looking at the masks the superheroes were wearing. "Could one of them be the Masked Messenger?" he whis-pered to himself.

"Electro-Melon, could you tell us why listening is so important?" Bok Choy asked.

"Certainly! Even though we're all superheroes with super gadgets and super powers, we don't know everything there is to know," he said. "We can always learn from someone else, whether they're young or old."

"That's right, EM. Very good," Bok Choy said. "Everyone

can teach us something."

Larryboy continued looking around the class and found something very disturbing: There was not just one super-hero with the letters M.M. on his mask... there were two! Oh no!

Bok Choy continued the lesson. "The second part of that message is to let the discerning get guidance. That means we also need to be careful to whom we listen. Raisinboy, would you care to elaborate on that?"

"Yes sir! That means it's important to listen to those who want what's best for us. People like our parents, our teachers, and God, to name a few."

"Good answer, Raisinboy. It's also important that we can *trust* the people to whom we listen."

CHAPTER 10

LOOKING FOR M. AND M. AND GOING PLAIN NUTS

Larryboy was worried. How would he ever be able to figure out which superhero with an M.M. on their mask was the real Masked Marvel? He'd have to talk to them, but how could he do that with Bok Choy in the room? Bok Choy would probably catch him talking, and Larryboy didn't want to have to go stand in the corner again. That dunce hat really clashed with his costume!

Suddenly, Larryboy had an idea. He'd distract Bok Choy and get him out of the room. Then he could weed out the real villain.

Larryboy burst into the room, pretending to be in great distress. "Bok Choy! Bok Choy!" he cried. "There's a terrible emergency! Some superhero must act!"

All the superheroes sprang to their feet, ready for action.

"Um…no," said Larryboy. "Only Bok Choy can handle *this* emergency!"

"Why is that?" asked

Bok Choy. "There are plenty of capable superheroes here."

"Well, uh...um...I mean...oh! This emergency is taking place in the *teacher's lounge*! Only teachers are allowed in there! And...they're out of coffee!"

"Jumpin' Java!" shouted Bok Choy. "This is a caffeine catastrophe! You superheroes stay here! I'll take care of this!"

Bok Choy leaped onto his desk, struck a heroic pose, and uttered his personal heroic cry, "Bok-Bok-Bok-Bok-Bok Choy, away!" He then rushed from the room.

As soon as Bok Choy exited, Larryboy slid up to the first of the superheroes with an M.M. on his mask.

"Nice mask!" Larryboy said. "I'm Larryboy, the superhero right here in Bumblyburg. And you are?"

"Muskie Melon," said the superhero with M.M. on his mask.

"Oh, that explains the smell," Larryboy said, disappointed that he wasn't the Masked Messenger.

"Sorry, I'm a little ripe," Muskie explained. "I didn't have a chance to shower after my Tie-Bow class."

"Tie-Bow class?" Larryboy inquired.

"Yeah, some of us superheroes who wear capes were having trouble keeping them tied when we were chasing after villains," Muskie explained. "We learned some new bows that won't come undone as easily. And we also looked at some fascinating..."

"Yeah, yeah," said Larryboy. "Good to meet you. Gotta go."

Well, one down. That meant that the other hero must be the real villain.

CHAPTER 11

WHEN WELL-MEANING SUPERHEROES ATTACK

Larryboy quickly moved to another desk that was beside the other superhero with M.M. on her mask.

"Nifty mask," Larryboy said. "Is it new?"

"As a matter of fact, it is," she said. "My old one was a poly-blend and gave me a horrible rash, when I got hot chasing villains. This one is high-tech Cottonesque. Wicks away the perspiration."

"I get the *message*," Larryboy said with a wink, trying to trick his new prime suspect.

"Funny you should mention that," the unknown superhero replied. "I'm very good with messages."

"I bet you are," Larryboy said, standing slowly. "Well, here's a message from Larryboy! It's not nice to mess with the ears of Bumblyburg!" With that, Larryboy shot both of his super-suction ears at the masked potato! When the other superheroes heard the commotion, they instinctively activated all of their super-gadgets.

In a split second, the room was filled with

ropes, grappling hooks, nets, hoses, smoke, bungee cords, squid ink, foam, slingshots, boomerangs, and a saxophone.

Just then, Bok Choy re-entered the room. "Larryboy, there's plenty of coffee in the…" Then he saw the mess. "What's going on here?"

Larryboy spoke up. "I discovered a super-villian infiltrating our class! The Masked Messenger! Her evil plan was to interfere with the ability of our fine citizens to be good lis-

teners, thereby creating chaos and confusion!"

The potato was struggling to say something, but there was a super-suction ear covering her mouth.

"Let's not jump to conclusions," Bok Choy said. "We'll listen to what she has to say before you try to whip her into shape. Release the plungers!"

Larryboy released her, and the potato readjusted her mask. "I should have stayed in Boise where they understand

us spuds," she said. "I am *not* the Masked Messenger! I am the Mashed Marvel!"

The other superheroes gasped.

"When I said I was good with messages," she continued, "I meant that I'm good with *mental* messages. I can read minds with my super powers."

Yeah, I just bet you can, Larryboy thought.

"No, I really can," the Mashed Marvel replied. "If you would have been a *good listener*, Larryboy, none of this would have happened!"

The other superheroes nodded in agreement as they gathered their super-gadgets and Superhero Handbooks.

"I think we all learned a valuable lesson tonight," said Bok Choy. "Now let's go out and be good listeners! Class dismissed!"

CHAPTER 12

THE STENCHMAN AND HIS HENCHMAN

Larryboy sat at his desk. He felt horrible. He had caused all kinds of trouble by not being a good listener. Worst of all, he had lost the respect of his fellow superheroes.

"Chin up, Larryboy."

It was Awful Alvin the Onion. He had been in the class all along, disguised as Marineboy! Now he and Larryboy were the only ones left in the classroom. Most of the lights were off, except for a floor lamp sitting off to one side.

"So you had a tough night. It happens to all of us," said the disguised onion. "I'm sure the other superheroes will forget all about this…in 10 or 20 years."

"I feel so foolish," Larryboy said. "I wish I was a better listener!"

Awful Alvin had to suppress a giggle.

Larryboy was walking right into his trap! "I have just the thing for that," Awful Alvin said, feeling especially awful. "I made these devices specifically to help people listen."

Being careful to stand behind Larryboy, he reached into a large box on the floor and carefully lifted two glowing orbs—the Extreme Ear Wacks! "Just tilt your head back," he said to Larryboy. "You'll be a better listener in no time!"

Awful Alvin needed a little more light to make sure the Extreme Ear Wacks were placed securely. He reached over and pulled Lampy from his strategic position near the wall. Larryboy glanced up as the lamp came into view.

"Oh, hi, Lampy!" he said.

Larryboy's eyes went wide. "Lampy?"

But before he could react, Awful Alvin had attached the Extreme Ear Wacks to Larryboy's super suction ears.

Larryboy heard the squeal of high-pitched tones, like a

radio dial being tuned to a distant station. Now Larryboy saw the villain remove the stolen mask and costume he had been wearing. It was Awful Alvin.

"So, we meet again," said Awful Alvin.

"You ever hear of breath mints?" Larryboy asked the onion-scented villain. But he couldn't even hear his own words! Then, when the static and squealing stopped, he could only hear the sound of Awful Alvin's voice. "Now, Larryboy, you will hear only what *I* want you to hear! And you will ignore hearing all that is good," he snickered. "I may even have you sing the Awful Alvin theme song that I just finished. And it's not as awful as you might suspect!

"I thought you might be onto my plan," Awful Alvin explained. So I put the letters M.M. on the box to throw you off the trail."

Larryboy tried hard not to listen to Awful Alvin's words, even going so far as to try and figure out the words to the Awful Alvin theme song.

MORE THAN JUST AN ONION, HE'S A SUPER ONION SNEAK. HE'S A REALLY ROTTEN STINKER, SO YOU DON'T DANCE CHEEK TO CHEEK.

It was no use! The villain's words took over, and they were the only thing Larryboy could hear. He had to fight it. He had to think of a way to contact Archie and stop this heartless onion!

But how?

CHAPTER 13

OH, WHERE IS MY LARRYBOY?

The next morning, Archie
was beside himself with worry. Larry's
jammies were neatly folded, his bunny
slipper was next to his bed, and his hair-
brush was right there in plain sight. It was
clear that Larry had not come home after superhero class last night.

Archie got no answer on any of Larryboy's com-
munication devices—not his Mop Video-Phone, not his
Belt-Buckle Radio, not his Transistor-Toaster Pastry, and
not even on his Digital Toothpick. Archie feared that
Larryboy was in the clutches of the Masked Messenger!
He called Bok Choy at the Bumblyburg Community
College and listened as the professor told him all about
the unfortunate incident that happened during superhero class. "So is it possible Larryboy could just be too
embarrassed to come home?" Archie asked.

"That could be," Bok Choy said. "But at least he
had someone to talk to. When I left, he was with
the superhero from Bumbly Bay, Marineboy!"

Archie thanked Bok Choy and turned his attention to the police scanner for possible news of Larryboy's whereabouts.

"Bumblyburg Station, this is car 54."

"Car 54, where are you?"

"We're on the outskirts of Bumblyburg in the Villain's Lair district. We just picked up this avocado we found wandering around here. You're not going to believe this, but guacamole here claims to be a kidnapped superhero from Bumbly Bay. He won't reveal his superhero identity, but he says his costume was stolen by Awful Alvin the Onion."

At that point, Archie put it all together: Larryboy was seen last with Marineboy, who is from Bumbly Bay. Then a superhero from Bumbly Bay claimed Awful Alvin had stolen his costume. Awful Alvin must have been posing as Marineboy when Bok Choy last saw Larryboy!

"Great galloping galoshes!" said Archie. "Larryboy must have fallen into the *awful* clutches of Awful Alvin the Onion…and Lampy."

Meanwhile, in the skies above Bumblyburg, an onion-shaped blimp positioned itself over the Veggie Valley Elementary School. In the blimp's gondola were Awful Alvin, Lampy, Larryboy, and hundreds of small velvet boxes rigged with tiny, tear-shaped parachutes.

Normally, Larryboy would have been uncomfortable at this height. And by "uncomfortable," I mean downright loopy with fear. Normally, he would have been curled up on the floor, calling out for his rubber duckie. But this was not a normal time for Larryboy. He was not acting like himself. He was acting less like a superhero and more like an un-superhero. His eyes were half-closed, and his mind could only register the constant villainous cackling of Awful Alvin.

"Prepare to watch the beginning of the end of the beginning that ends the begin … well, just watch!" said Awful Alvin. "Each of these precious parachutes will carry a pair of Ear Wacks to the unsuspecting playground below."

When the kids at Veggie Valley place the Ear Wacks in their ears, Awful Alvin knew they would only be able to hear one thing…his own hideous commands! The kids would become his drones, just like Larryboy…except without plunger ears.

"We are over the drop site!" Awful Alvin announced. "Lampy! Release the Ear Wacks!"

Lampy stood straight and remained very still.

"This is no time for second thoughts, Lampy. Ear Wacks away!"

Lampy's shade moved slightly in the breeze, but the trap door beneath the boxes remained closed. "You're right, Lampy," he said. "Maybe we should let our special guest have the honor. Larryboy! Pull the lever and drop the Ear Wacks down to the school children of Veggie Valley!"

Under the control of the Extreme Ear Wacks and Awful Alvin's villainous voice, Larryboy pulled the lever and released the Ear Wacks to fall to the children of Veggie Valley Elementary School.

CHAPTER 14

THE EAR WAX UNRAVELS

Back at the Larry-Cave, Archie paced nervously back and forth. Suddenly, the Larry-Alarm went off! The Larry-Radar had detected an unknown object in the skies above Bumblyburg!

"To the Larry-Scope" yelled Archie.

Archie blushed, as he realized there was no one there other than Larry's rubber duckie. He was talking to himself again.

Archie regained his composure and pressed a button, which caused a high-power telescope to emerge from one of the turrets on the mansion. It was a clear day, and it didn't take long to spot the slow-moving, onion-shaped blimp in the sky over Bumblyburg.

Archie zoomed in on the blimp. "Oh my, Master Larry," Archie said as he saw Larryboy standing next to Awful Alvin. "What has he done to you?" Then, Archie noticed Larryboy's glassy-eyed stare and the glowing orbs in his ears. He zoomed in on the orbs with full magnification. He could make out

several small words. **"IF...YOU...CAN...READ...THIS, ...YOU... HAVE...A...REALLY...GOOD...TELESCOPE!"**

Then he pulled back a little on the zoom function and read the larger letters: "Extreme Ear Wacks."

Ear Wacks! Suddenly, Archie realized why Larryboy hadn't been responding on his communicator. He was under the control of the Ear Wacks.

"This is terrible!" said Archie. "Those Ear Wacks are extremely powerful! If I don't find a way to neutralize them quickly, the damage could become permanent!"

Archie took the smaller set of Ear Wacks that Larryboy had given him down to the Larry-Lab. He had to study them to find a way to disarm the Ear Wacks! The future of Bumblyburg was at stake!

Meanwhile, back at Veggie Valley Elementary, Awful

Alvin's plan was working perfectly. Junior Asparagus was running around trying to warn his classmates not to put the Ear Wacks in their ears. But none of them were listening. The kids were excited at the prospect of only hearing what *they* wanted to hear.

But instead of hearing only what they wanted to hear, the kids ended up hearing something no one wanted to hear: The *awful* voice of Awful Alvin! They became unwilling servants, just like Larryboy. The kids surrounded Junior, and soon, even *he* had Ear Wacks in his ears.

Alvin's blimp landed on the playground. "Touch down!" he said. "Seven points for us, Lampy! Or is it six? What does it matter? I make the rules now, and I say it's seven! Let's get some cheerleaders. Maybe a mascot, too. An onion ring might be nice. Go rings! It has a nice 'ring' to it, don't you think, Lampy? **HA HA HA HA!**"

Normally, Larryboy would have taken Awful Alvin to jail just for making such a bad pun. But all he could do now was listen through the Extreme Ear Wacks.

"Okay, my faithful kiddie brigade," Awful Alvin said to the Ear-Wacked children of Veggie Valley Elementary. "It's time for you to do my bidding! And I bid that you shall do *awful* things that will please me, and only me!"

Then Awful Alvin looked at Larryboy and explained how the children of Bumblyburg were now under *his* control. "I've taken away the authority of anyone they've ever listened to…parents, teachers, police officers…even God! They are all powerless in the eyes…I mean ears…of the children! **HA HA HA HA!**" he cackled.

He had the kids line up and started giving them awful commands that only Awful Alvin's awful mind could ever have come up with. First, he commanded them to stand on their heads. Then he commanded them to hop around like kangaroos. After that, he commanded them to scratch that spot on his back that he could never reach.

Then, he commanded them to do something so awful that it was almost *too awful* for even Awful Alvin. He commanded them to…*country line dance!*

Larryboy and the Veggie Valley kids could only helplessly obey each of the commands.

CHAPTER 15

ARCHIE MAKES AN EERIE, WACKY DISCOVERY

Meanwhile, back at the Larry-Cave, Archie was working feverishly to find a way to disable the Ear Wacks, but nothing was working. Picking up a tiny Ear Wack, Archie carried it over to the electron microscope, passing near the communications console.

As he did, an ear-piercing screech echoed through the Larry-Cave. In the gondola of the blimp, Larryboy heard the same screech, only louder! Awful Alvin heard it, too, EVEN LOUDER, due to the microchips implanted in his inner ears.

"OWWW!" Archie shrieked in the Larry-Cave.

"YOUCH!!" Larryboy yelped in the blimp's gondola.

"OUCHIE-WAWAAAAA!!!" Awful Alvin screamed.

Achie flipped off the microphone switch, and everything went silent. "I must have left the microphone on when I last attempted to call Master Larry," he mumbled to himself. "That screech was audio feedback from the microphone."

Archie had accidentally discovered a way to communicate to the Ear Wacks! With some extra fine-tuning, maybe he could reach Larryboy. But how could he counter the effect of the Extreme Ear Wacks?

That part would have to be up to Larryboy. Only Larryboy could listen and learn by stopping to think about what he was hearing and from whom. He would have to discern whom he trusted and who was telling him what was best for him. And that certainly wasn't Awful Alvin.

When the ringing in his ears subsided, Larryboy thought he'd heard Archie's distinctive voice. It sounded like he had said, **"OWWW!"**

To Awful Alvin, it had sounded like the ringing of a thousand bells—a thousand bells that went 'Owww.' When he could hear again at last, he said, "Lampy! Shed some light on this problem! What caused that malfunction? I want some answers *now*!"

CHAPTER 16

THE EVIL HAS LANDED

Lampy provided no answers. But he didn't
claim there was any further threat, either. So long
as the Veggie kids continued to follow Alvin's orders,
everything seemed to be going according to plans.

"No one can stop me now!" Awful Alvin screeched.
"Now Larryboy will be using his super-powers to help
me do any awful thing I choose—like taking cuts in
lines at the movies, checking out with more than ten
items in the express lane, driving alone in the car
pool lane, swimming without a life guard at the
community pool, and tearing off those "Do Not
Remove" labels on mattresses. The list is endless!"

Picking up his Ear Wacks transmitter, Awful
Alvin announced, "Children of Bumblyburg! It's
time for more of your Awful Assignments.
The reign of Awful Alvin the Onion is
about to begin! HA HA HA HA
HA HA!"

The villain's maniacal laugh was still ringing in Larryboy's ears when he once again heard high-pitched squeals. Suddenly, Awful Alvin's voice seemed to be mixing with Archie's. If there was ever a time Larryboy needed guidance, it was now!

Larryboy thought back to the lesson he'd heard in his superhero class. He realized he had been listening in class, but he hadn't really paid attention. He thought hard. *Let the wise...something...and get guidance. Or was it guide the wise to avoid something ... ? Maybe "Get the rice pudding if you have a yearning." That doesn't seem right either.*

Larryboy focused all his concentration on the lesson, and finally, not only the words came to him, but the meaning! "Let the wise listen and add to their learning, and let the discerning get guidance."

He just had to listen to the people he trusted, those who loved him and wanted what was best for him. Suddenly, it became perfectly clear and he could hear only Archie!

"Master Larry," Archie said quietly. "If you truly learned your lesson, you should be able to hear me. I have a plan. Now, listen carefully."

Archie went through the plan with Larryboy, who carefully listened to the guidance from his trusted butler and mentor. The superhero knew it was his only chance to defeat Awful Alvin and save Bumblyburg. He had to break the spell of the Ear Wacks once and for all!

CHAPTER 17

EVIL ON THE INSIDE, CHEWY ON THE OUTSIDE

Grabbing a list of student names he had stolen from Veggie Valley Elementary School, Awful Alvin began giving out awful assignments. "Percy Pea! You're going to be in charge of putting 'Wet Paint' signs on all benches, bushes, doors, sidewalks, trees, and streets. Okay. Hop to it." Percy nodded and moved to obey.

"Laura Carrot!" he called. "You will be in charge of mixing the recyclables with the regular garbage. Go on, now."

Awful Alvin continued giving out Awful Assignments to all the kids—drinking directly out of milk cartons at the grocery store, replacing #2 pencils with #3's, breaking the bottom tips off pointed ice cream cones, losing the caps to colored markers—until only Junior Asparagus remained.

"Ah, Junior Asparagus, my little green friend. I have an *especially* awful job for you," cackled Awful Alvin.

Junior snapped to action, but instead of listening to Awful Alvin, he concentrated on what he had heard from his mom and dad. They had taught him to listen only to the people who loved him—the people he could trust. This was his chance to help Larryboy! "I won't listen to you, Mr. Awful! I'm only going to listen to the people who care about me. You care about me, don't you Larryboy?"

Junior's words got through to Larryboy loud and clear.

"I sure do, Junior! Bumblyburg is in need of a hero, and **I AM THAT HERO!**"

Taking aim at Awful Alvin, he fired both super-suction ears in rapid succession. Unfortunately, they fell to the ground and bounced at the villain's feet. "Uh-oh," Larryboy said.

"Did you really think I wouldn't deactivate your firing mechanism?" Awful Alvin asked. "Please, Larryboy. Give me a little more credit than that."

"Well, I have plenty of other weapons to use against you!" Larryboy said. "Don't I, Archie? Oh, I forgot he can't hear me unless I turn this on."

Larryboy activated his Belt Buckle radio and a tremendous screech of feedback filled the air. Luckily for Larryboy, the Extreme Ear Wacks no longer had any effect.

Unluckily for Awful Alvin, his inner-ear implants were still cranked to the max. He clutched his ears in pain, but he managed to get out one command.

"Children, seize him! Switch off his Belt Buckle radio!" he cried. The kids dutifully surrounded Larryboy!

"No, wait!" the superhero protested. "Kids, it's *me*, Larryboy! Listen to me. Don't you trust me? You know I want what's best for all of you! You have to choose very carefully when you decide to whom you will listen. I'm the good guy. *He's* the bad guy, and he doesn't want to do what's right!"

As Junior switched off Larryboy's Belt Buckle radio, he looked up at his hero and realized that he trusted Larryboy. Larryboy loved him and wanted what was best for him. Awful Alvin did not!

As Junior understood the value of listening to the right people, he was able to shake his head hard enough to cause the Ear Wacks to fall out! He smiled at Larryboy and looked around at the other kids. Percy Pea grinned as he too listened to Larryboy. Then Laura Carrot smiled as the superhero's words came through loud and clear.

Two by two, the Ear Wacks were shaken out of the kids' ears, and everybody realized just how awful Awful Alvin was. As the villain slowly recovered from his latest bout with the screeching feedback, Larryboy quickly hatched a plan.

"Does everyone have chewing gum?" he whispered to the kids. The kids took an assortment of gum from their pockets: Squiggly's Spearmint, Palooka Pop, Molar Madness, Chewy Kablooey, Gooeylicious, Jaw Mashers, Tooth Tinglers.

Every kind of gum imaginable!

"Get chewing!" Larryboy said quietly, as Awful Alvin struggled back to a standing position. "When you get a good, sticky wad, take out your Ear Wacks, stick 'em in the gum, and stick the gum to Awful Alvin."

Everyone started chewing frantically, including Larryboy, who gobbled a whole pack of his favorite grape gum, Bubblyburst.

Awful Alvin's head was still throbbing as he turned to the kids.

"Listen up, children!" he commanded. "Okay, I tricked you into wearing the Ear Wacks. But that doesn't mean you still can't listen to me. In fact, if you listen to me now, you will get to help me mess up the entire school! Doesn't that sound like fun? No more school?"

The kids paused. Messing up the school *did* sound like fun. But before the kids could do anything, Junior said, "Larryboy's right! Awful Alvin is a *bad* guy! If we listen to *him*, we'll end up doing bad stuff, too! We need to listen to those who care about us! Those who care about doing what's right...like Larryboy!"

Junior Asparagus smiled at Larryboy, and Larryboy smiled right back.

Awful Alvin, however, did not smile. Especially when a glistening hunk of pink Palooka Pop hit him squarely on the forehead and stuck tight.

"Who threw that?" Awful Alvin demanded, as a bluish wad of Molar Madness hit his cheek and three other soggy pieces of assorted chewing gum landed on his head. "Lampy! Help me!" the villain cried. But even his faithful friend seemed not to hear.

The kids were determined to bring this villain down by attacking him with colored wads of gum, each with tiny, blinking Ear Wacks inside.

"Stop it! Stop it right now!" Alvin said, slowly realizing deep down in his stinky layers that the Ear Wacks weren't working anymore. He backed away slowly, grabbing Lampy and looking for an escape route.

As Awful Alvin tried to run to his blimp to get away, Larryboy stuck two extremely large wads of purple gum on either side of the villain's head. Two orb-shaped wads of gum glowed and caused a slight tremor in the air.

The Extreme Ear Wacks were no longer in Larryboy's

84

super-suction ears. They were embedded in the grape gum
stuck to Awful Alvin's head, along with hundreds of smaller
Ear Wacks stuck all over him.

"I have a little feedback for you, Awful Alvin,"
Larryboy said. "First of all, don't mess with Bumblyburg.
Second of all...this."

Larryboy reached down and switched on his Belt Buckle
radio. In that very instant, an onion-splitting pitch of feedback emitted from hundreds of Ear Wacks, plus the Extreme
Ear Wacks from Larryboy, launching Awful Alvin and Lampy
high into the air over Bumblyburg!

A billowing trail of steam followed Alvin and Lampy as
they landed with a splash in the community swimming pool.

"Anyone for onion dip?" Larryboy quipped as the citizens of Bumblyburg cheered!

CHAPTER 18

THERE'S NO TASTE LIKE LIVER AND NO PLACE LIKE HOME

"It's good to be home, Archie," Larry said as he relaxed in his favorite easy chair. "And it's good to have Bumblyburg back to normal."

"Indeed it is," said Archie.

"I sure did learn a valuable lesson about listening," Larry said.

"That's good news!" said Archie. "Because I was just going to tell you that it is time for you to get back to your janitor job."

Suddenly, a glassy look came over Larry's eyes. "What was that, Archie? I can't *hear* you. Those Ear Wacks must be affecting me again!"

Archie put a big piece of chewing gum into his mouth and began to chew. "Master Larry," he said. "I have a big wad of Bubblyburst, and I'm not afraid to use it!"

Larry hopped up out of his chair. "Heh heh. I was just kidding! Just *kidding*!" he said as he grabbed his mop and rushed off to work.

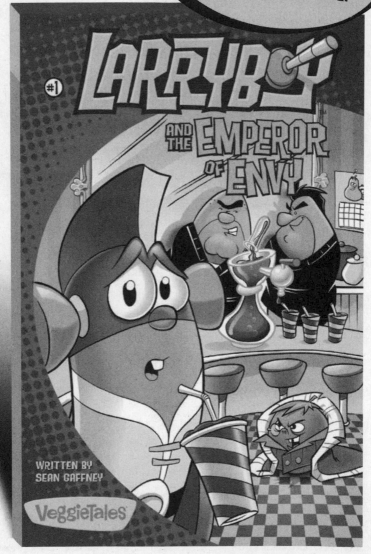

SOFTCOVER ISBN 978-0-310-70467-6

CHAPTER 1

SOMETHING ROTTEN IN THE SCHOOL OF BUMBLYBURG

It was a typical day at Bumblyburg's Veggie Valley Elementary School. Well, okay, maybe it wasn't such a typical day. In fact, something just plain weird was going on. The teacher, Mr. Asparagus, was acting a bit oddly.

"Don't you think Mr. Asparagus is acting a bit oddly?" asked Lenny Carrot about his teacher.

"He sure is," said Laura Carrot. "And he looks kind of funny. Like cardboard."

"His lips don't move when he talks," Percy Pea piped in. "That's weird."

"You know," said Renee Blueberry, "he looks a bit like a scallion from the side."

"What do you think, Junior?" asked Laura.

Junior Asparagus didn't know what to think! After all, the teacher was his father. But his dad was acting oddly. And he sure did look funny. Almost as if he was wearing a cardboard mask drawn with crayon.

"Time for a math lesson," squeaked the teacher.

"See!" whispered Percy. "His lips didn't move!"

"That doesn't sound like my dad," said Junior.

The teacher put a black bag on top of his desk. "Now, children," the teacher said, "I want you all to put your milk money into this bag. Then we will play a game."

"What game?" asked Junior.

"Hide-and-Seek," replied the teacher. "You will close your eyes and count to a million while I run and hide. Won't that be fun?"

Junior thought hard. His dad sounded funny, looked as if he was wearing a cardboard mask, talked without moving his lips, and now asked the kids to hand over their milk money for a game of Hide-and-Seek.

"Hey!" shouted Junior. "You aren't my dad! You're the Milk Money Bandit!"

"But I look like your dad, don't you think?" asked the teacher.

"I think you're wearing a mask," said Junior.

"Am not," said the teacher.

"Are too!"

"Am not!"

At that moment, a rather large suction cup flew through the open window and plopped onto Mr. Asparagus' face. With a loud *THWOOP*, the plunger was pulled back through the window, ripping off the mask. It was the Milk Money Bandit after all!

"Erk!" shrieked the Bandit.

"I knew it!" exclaimed Junior. "But where did that plunger come from?"

All the students turned and looked out the window. It

was Larryboy! One of his suction-cup ears sported the Milk Money Bandit's mask, and he was trying to shake it loose.

"I am that hero!" Larryboy proclaimed.

Then Larryboy leaped through the open window, tripped on the windowsill, and fell into the classroom, landing on his face.

"I meant to do that," the hero said, popping upright. "Now, Bandit, where is the *real* Mr. Asparagus? Talk now, unless you want the other ear!"

Larryboy leaned threateningly toward the bandit.

"No, not the ears! I'll talk!" howled the villain. "I just

wish I had more milk money!"

Larryboy scowled at the bandit.

"Mr. Asparagus is in the closet!" the bandit said, quickly.

Junior ran to the closet and opened the door.

"Dad!"

"Son!"

Junior's dad hopped out of the closet.

"It sure was dark in there," Mr. Asparagus said. "Thank you, Junior."

Mr. Asparagus came out of the closet and looked at the Milk Money Bandit quite sternly. "*You* should learn to be content with the money you have!" he scolded. "Thank *you*, Larryboy, for saving the day!"

Larryboy smiled. "My pleasure," he said. "And now to take care of the bandit!"

LARRYBOY AND THE SINISTER SNOW DAY
Written by Sean Gaffney

Bumblyburg is in danger of becoming a frozen wasteland! The Veggie kids want a snow day because they think school is boring. Does Larryboy think so, too? Can he convince himself and show everyone that when you stop learning, you stop growing? Will he be able to hamper Iceburg and his notorious band of snow peas' sinister plot before Bumblyburg plunges to an icy doom?

SOFTCOVER ISBN 978-0-310-70561-1

BOOK #4
IN A STORE
NEAR YOU!

LARRYBOY AND THE YODELNAPPER
Written by Kent Redeker

Larryboy goes undercover as a world-famous yodeler
to foil the scheme of Green Greta, the greedy zucchini,
who is kidnapping yodelers out of greed. Things go
from bad to worse when Larryboy tries to capture Greta
and is attacked by an entire collection of Hula dolls.
Instead of being frightened, Larryboy sees this as a
chance to complete his own Hula doll set. But does he
really need them all? Will he realize how to be content?

SOFTCOVER ISBN 978-0-310-70562-8

#2

AND THE AWFUL EAR WACKS ATTACKS

Ear wacks have attacked Bumblyburg! Larryboy's fiendish nemesis, Alvin the Onion, is behind it and has unleashed the awful ear wacks to interfere with being a good listener. When Larryboy falls into Alvin's awful trap and he can no longer listen, it's up to Junior Asparagus and Larryboy's faithful butler and mentor, Archie, to foil the evil plot.

What will come of Bumblyburg now that their superhero is under Alvin's awful spell? Will Junior and Archie be able to convince Larryboy to listen to them in time to save Bumblyburg? Will Larryboy's super-suction ears be saturated with evil for all time? Alvin's out to rule the city and Larryboy forever!

BOB KATULA is an advertising and marketing freelance writer and has written a biography of popular American artist Terry Redlin. He finds inspiration in his wife and two daughters.

JUVENILE FICTION / Religious / General

USD $4.99

ISBN 978-0-310-70468-3

5 0 4 9 9

9 780310 704683

ZONDERkidz™
.com

BIG IDEA
bigidea.com